MW00897722

For our wild animals

Written by: Nathan Dye
Illustrated by: Chris Dye

Constance is a peahen who
lives in the Cincinnati Zoo.

Peahens are female Peafowls.
Peacocks are male Peafowls.

Peahens are one of the few animals allowed to roam free around people..

Every day Constance walks through the zoo, watching people take pictures with her more beautiful peacock friends.

Since she doesn't have a big beautiful train of
feathers, most kids don't pay attention to her.

Constance always wished she were
more beautiful like her friend Vale.

All the kids just love Vale.

No matter how many times Vale told Constance
she was beautiful...she never believed him.

She has never experienced the shimmering teal, gold,
blue and silver colors the way most peacocks do.

One evening, when Constance got home
from a long day, she looked in the mirror,
and she didn't like what she saw.

It made her sad.
So sad she started cry.

Just then, she remembered a song her mom
used to sing to her when she was sad.

At that moment,
Constance started to sing
the most beautiful song.

She started off quietly, but as her voice grew louder, her confidence started to rise...

Her voice carried
across the entire zoo.

When she had finished,
Constance opened her eyes
to see all the animals in the
zoo watching her sing her
beautiful song.

They asked her to
sing again for them.

At first, she was very shy, but as she
started to sing, her confidence grew.

From that day forward, Constance sang her beautiful
songs, and the crowds would always gather.

It made her feel so happy, and so proud, that
she had found her beauty from within.

This is a story about finding your beauty.
Sometimes it's outward facing and
sometimes it's something that comes from
within, but each of us has something that
makes us beautiful in our own way.

CPSIA information can be obtained
at www.ICGtesting.com
Printed in the USA
LVHW050832110322
713183LV00008B/140

9 780578 446899